LOLLOPY

JD – For Rebecca Jane

This edition published in 1999 by Diamond Books
77–85 Fulham Palace Road,
Hammersmith, London, W6 8JB

First published in Great Britain by Andersen Press Ltd in 1991
First published in Picture Lions in 1993
10 9 8 7 6 5 4 3 2 1
Picture Lions is an imprint of the Children's Division, part of HarperCollins Publishers Limited,
77–85 Fulham Palace Road, Hammersmith, London W6 8JB

ISBN 0 261 67165 0

Printed and bound in Slovenia

LOLLOPY

Written by
JOYCE DUNBAR

Illustrated by
SUSAN VARLEY

CARNIVAL

IT was bluebell time in the wood. Sophie wasn't allowed to walk there alone so she took her toy rabbit with her.
Sophie's toy rabbit had long, lollopy ears and long, lollopy arms and long, lollopy legs.

Sophie called him Lollopy.

"CAN you see the bluebells?" she said, lifting his big heavy head so that he could see. She was sure that Lollopy nodded.

Sophie wandered further and further into the wood, where the bluebells grew thicker and thicker. She stopped to pick a bunch of bluebells. As she picked more and more, Lollopy slipped from her hands.

WHEN Sophie got home her mother put the bluebells in some water.

"They're lovely," she said, "but you know you musn't wander off into the wood by yourself."

"I didn't," said Sophie. "I took Lollopy, and - oh! I've lost him!" Sophie was nearly in tears.

"Don't worry," said her mother. "We'll look for him tomorrow."

THE moon came up in the sky. Lollopy's head hung down. When the rabbits tried to come out of their burrow, they found something in the way.

"It's the Bogey-Rabbit!" said Twitch.

"He's come to take us away!" said Tinker.

"He's going to eat us all up!" said Snuff.

"Nonsense," said their mother and nudged her way past. Lollopy slumped over on his side. All the rabbits came out to look.

"What is it?" asked Snuff.

"Is it alive?" asked Twitch. Mother Rabbit lifted Lollopy's ears so that she could see into his eyes. Sophie understood his eyes. So did Mother Rabbit.

"He's Lollopy!" she said. "And he's lost."

"We'll look after him," said her children. "He can join in our games."

B ᴜᴛ when they tried to play hide-and-seek with him, Lollopy just lolloped in a heap. And when they played rough-and-tumble, he lolled about, any old how. Even when they teased him, Lollopy took no notice. They decided he was no fun at all!

"I know what would make him jump," said Tinker. The others looked at him, wide-eyed.

"Not the Bogey-Rabbit!" said Twitch.

"We wouldn't dare," whispered Snuff. But they knew they were going to try.

WHILE their mother was dozing, they carried Lollopy into the wood. Further and further they went, into the deepest, darkest middle, where the big bad Bogey-Rabbit lurked. There was silence and stillness all around.

"What does he look like?" asked Twitch.

"How will we know if it's him?" said Snuff. All of them shivered with fear.

"Look! The Bogey-Rabbit's ears!" whispered Snuff.
"Look! The Bogey-Rabbit's eyes!" murmured Twitch.
"Help! The Bogey-Rabbit's teeth!" yelped Tinker.

And the rabbits ran all the way home!

"WHERE have you *been*?" said their mother. "You know you musn't wander off by yourselves."
"The Bogey-Rabbit got Lollopy!" they said.
"We didn't mean it!"
"We were only playing!"
"We just wanted to make him jump!"

THEY found Lollopy the next morning. He did look a sorry sight.

"It wasn't a Bogey-Rabbit that got him," said their mother. "But it might have been a fox and it might have got one of you instead. You're not so easy to mend."

She sewed Lollopy's ear back on and patched up his leg. Her children made him a dandelion medal on a bluebell chain, because they were sorry, and because he had been so brave. Then they left him, sitting by a tree.

IT was Sophie's mother who saw him first but it was Sophie who picked him up.

"Look at his ear and his leg!" she said.

"He's had an accident," said her mother. "But who could have patched him up?"

"And who made him a bluebell chain?" said Sophie, giving him a great big hug. And Sophie told Lollopy never to go into the wood again, not even if she went with him.

A<small>ND</small> he never did.

Joyce Dunbar was born in Scunthorpe, Lincolnshire in 1944. She attended Goldsmiths College at London University and then spent twenty years teaching English and Art. Now a full-time writer, Joyce has written novels for children as well as picture books. She now lives in Norwich with her husband, James, who is an illustrator and toy-maker, their two children and numerous pets.

Born in Blackpool in 1961, Susan Varley obtained a BA in graphic design from Manchester Polytechnic. Her tutor there was Tony Ross, the well-known illustrator of children's picture books. Susan's first book was BADGER'S PARTING GIFTS which she wrote to help children get over the death of someone they love. It won the prestigious *Mother Goose Award* in 1985 and is currently available in Picture Lions. Susan has continued to illustrate many successful picture books.